Pippen Island

Written by Michaela Morgan

Illustrated by Nathalie Ortega

Collins

Who and what is in this story?

Listen and say

Dad

Billy

🎧 The family were on an adventure to Pippen Island.

There they are: Mum, Dad, Milly and Billy … and little Mo.

There's the boat. Ready for the island adventure!

It's my birthday!

Milly was very happy and excited.
It was her birthday!
Billy was very happy and excited, too.

It's an adventure!

Little Mo was afraid. The waves were very big.
The sea was VERY big and ...

"That fish is very big," Mo said, "Aah!
It's a shark!"

"Don't be afraid. It's only a big fish.
Look!" said Mum.

"Look. A crocodile!" Mo said.

"It's only a tree!" said Dad. "Don't worry."
But little Mo did worry.

"Here's the island," said Mum.

"I have a present for you, Milly" she said,
"Look ..."

It was a map.

Milly needed to find the things on the map and then look behind the rock.

Pippen Island

Ten Steps and Look behind the rock

big rock

tree

X

N

sea

E

W

S

The children started their walk.
"There's the forest." said Billy.

"What's that noise?" asked Mo.
"It's only the wind," said Milly.
"Don't worry."

"There's the river!" said Billy.

"I can feel an animal ... " said Mo.

"What is it? Mice? Bees? A lion?!"

"It's nothing," said Billy.

"But I can see white!" said Mo.

Milly smiled. "That's only a tree," she said.
"There's the big rock. We take ten steps.
One, two, three, four, five, six, seven,
eight, nine, ten ... and go behind the rock
and what do we find?"

A birthday picnic!

And presents and birthday cards and games and books – and a kite!

"Let's play with the kite now," said Dad, "and then we can have our picnic."

They had a nice time, but back at the picnic ...

"Oh no!" said Mo, "What's that? A goat?"

"My birthday cards! My picnic!" said Milly,
"My hat! My socks!" said Dad.

"There is *some* food," said Mum,
"And the cake is here! Let's sing
Happy Birthday."

They sang to Milly. "I have an idea for a
song," said Milly, "Mo, you just say 'NO!'"

Do snakes eat cakes?
No!

Do mice eat rice?
No!

Do bees eat cheese?
No!

Do cats eat hats?
No!

Are the socks behind
the rocks?
No!

What's that? Is it
a goat?
Yes!

Picture dictionary

Listen and repeat

bee
birthday card

goat

lion

map

mice

rock

shark

smile

snake

wave

1 Look and order the story

2 Listen and say

Collins

Published by Collins
An imprint of HarperCollins*Publishers*
Westerhill Road
Bishopbriggs
Glasgow
G64 2QT

HarperCollins*Publishers*
1st Floor, Watermarque Building
Ringsend Road
Dublin 4
Ireland

William Collins' dream of knowledge for all began with the publication of his first book in 1819.

A self-educated mill worker, he not only enriched millions of lives, but also founded a flourishing publishing house. Today, staying true to this spirit, Collins books are packed with inspiration, innovation and practical expertise. They place you at the centre of a world of possibility and give you exactly what you need to explore it.

10 9 8 7 6 5 4 3 2

ISBN 978-0-00-839710-4

Collins® and COBUILD® are registered trademarks of HarperCollins*Publishers* Limited

www.collins.co.uk/elt

British Library Cataloguing in Publication Data

A catalogue record for this publication is available from the British Library.

Author: Michaela Morgan
Illustrator: Nathalie Ortega (Beehive)
Series editor: Rebecca Adlard
Commissioning editor: Fiona Undrill and Zoë Clarke
Publishing manager: Lisa Todd
Product managers: Jennifer Hall and Caroline Green
In-house editor: Alma Puts Keren
Project manager: Emily Hooton
Editor: Frances Amrani
Proofreaders: Natalie Murray and Michael Lamb
Cover designer: Kevin Robbins
Typesetter: 2Hoots Publishing Services Ltd
Audio produced by id audio, London
Reading guide author: Emma Wilkinson
Production controller: Rachel Weaver
Printed and bound by: GPS Group, Slovenia

MIX
Paper from responsible sources

FSC
www.fsc.org

FSC™ C007454

This book is produced from independently certified FSC™ paper to ensure responsible forest management.

For more information visit: **www.harpercollins.co.uk/green**

Download the audio for this book and a reading guide for parents and teachers at www.collins.co.uk/839710